YOUR FAVOURITE
FIREMAN SAM
STORY COLLECTION

DEAN

Contents

Sam's Brass Band   6

A Spot of Bother   13

All in a Good Cause   20

Lost in the Fog   27

The Fairground Rescue   34

Norman and the Runaway Cow   41

Penny's First Aid Drill   48

James and the Well   55

Sam's Brass Band

"Come on, Uncle Sam, we'll challenge you to a game of cricket," said James one hot Saturday morning.

"Oh yes, good idea, it's a perfect day for cricket," Sarah agreed.

"Well, all right then," Fireman Sam replied, "but I can't stay long - I'm meeting the others for band practice later."

Fireman Sam went into bat, with James bowling and Sarah looking out for a catch.

Trevor was doing some weeding in his garden next door.

"I'm getting old, boyo," he said, standing up and stretching. Before he knew what was happening, a cricket ball landed in his upturned hand. "But I haven't lost my eye for the ball!"

"Oi, someone's out for a duck!" Trevor called over the fence. "Oh sorry, Sam," he said sheepishly. "Didn't realise it was you."

"Never mind," Fireman Sam replied. "It's your turn now, Trevor. I'm off to band practice - we're doing a special concert tomorrow."

"What's that, Norman?" asked Fireman Sam when he called at Dilys's shop.

"It's Dad's old telescope. Want a look?" Norman grinned.

"Powerful telescope this is, Norman. I can see as far as Jupiter!" joked Fireman Sam as he looked through the telescope. Norman didn't say anything.

"Hey, Norman, I said I can see Jup . . ." Fireman Sam repeated. Norman roared with laughter and ran out.

"It wasn't that funny Norman!"

"Hello Sam," said Dilys. "Ooo! How did you get a black eye?"

"Probably the same way you did, Dilys!"

"Boot polish!" exclaimed Dilys.

"Glad to see Norman hasn't lost his sense of humour," Fireman Sam laughed.

"Norman Price, come back here!" shrieked Dilys.

Back in Fireman Sam's garden, Trevor was still batting.

"Just wait, Mr Evans," thought James as he bowled the ball.

WHAM! The ball flew up onto the roof and lodged itself next to the chimney.

"OK, Mr Evans, you've won," sighed Sarah. "That's the end of the game."

"I must get your ball back first. I'll use this," shouted Trevor. He grabbed an old ladder, leaned it against the house and began to climb up.

"Uh oh! That ladder's ancient and I seem to remember Trevor and ladders don't mix," said Sarah, watching from below.

"Help! I forgot, I can't stand heights!" Trevor squeaked from the top of the ladder.

"Come down the ladder then, Mr Evans," called James.

"Not until I've got your ball," said Trevor bravely.

He scrambled onto the roof and reached out for the ball. Before he could grab it, the ball rolled off the roof, down the drainpipe and straight into James's hands.

"Out Trevor, at last!" cheered James.

"Just you wait!" Trevor said crossly. "I'm coming down."

But as he spun round, he slipped down the roof and kicked the ladder over. It fell to the ground and smashed to pieces.

"Now what shall we do?" gasped James.

"Well, don't just stand there, do something!" shouted Trevor, clinging to the guttering with his eyes closed. "I can't hang on much longer."

"I'll call the fire brigade," Sarah shouted. She ran inside Fireman Sam's house.

Up at the fire station, the Pontypandy Brass Band were practising for the concert.

"We're not very good are we?" grumbled Station Officer Steele, putting cotton wool in his ears.

9

"Practice makes perfect, Sir," said Penny.

"Once more then," Station Officer Steele sighed, picking up his baton.

"Fireman Cridlington, try to keep up with us," he bellowed above the noise.

Elvis smiled at Penny and fully extended the slide on his trombone. There was a loud crash and the band stopped playing.

Elvis had punctured Penny's drum!

"Tha . . . that's torn it, Sir," stuttered Elvis, blushing bright red.

"Drum's patched up, Sir. Ready when you are," said Penny Morris a few minutes later.

"Very well. After two – one, two."

But instead of the brass band, the fire alarm sounded.

"Action stations," Station Officer Steele cried.

"Fireman trapped on roof," read Penny. "It must be Trevor!"

"Firefighter Morris, deal with any other calls; everyone else, into Jupiter," ordered Station Officer Steele.

"Knowing Trevor's head for heights, we haven't got long," said Fireman Sam.

"Aargh! I'm falling!" Trevor yelled.

"Prepare ladders. Extend!" commanded Station Officer Steele.

Moving quickly, the fire brigade put the ladder against Fireman Sam's house.

"Thank goodness you're here, Uncle Sam," cried Sarah when they arrived. "Trevor's sliding off your roof!"

"Oh no, not the ladder," Trevor pleaded.

"Are you an Auxiliary Fireman or not, Evans?" snorted Station Officer Steele.

"Anything but the ladder," Trevor shuddered, looking over the edge.

"Come on, Trevor, you've done it before, remember?" Fireman Sam said kindly.

"That's what I'm worried about!"

"Don't look down, boyo," Trevor muttered to himself. "Just don't look down!"

Fireman Sam and Elvis looked at each other. "Hey, Trevor, it's Bella's special spaghetti bolognaise for supper tonight," Elvis called out.

Suddenly, Trevor slipped off the roof but managed to cling on to the ladder.

"I'm losing my appetite!" he moaned as he slid quickly down the ladder. "Ooooh," he wailed, landing with a bump in the middle of the firemen.

"Still haven't got the hang of it, have we, Evans?" Station Officer Steele remarked.

"Well, that's that problem solved, Sir!" said Fireman Sam.

"But what about the concert tomorrow?" said Station Officer Steele, looking worried. "I know practice makes perfect, but we haven't got much time."

"If I could have the afternoon in my inventing shed, I think we could be in with a chance."

Fireman Sam whispered his idea to Station Officer Steele as the rest of them lowered the ladder.

The next day at the concert in the park, the Pontypandy Brass Band were playing beautifully.

"Not bad, are they?" said Dilys.

"Too modest, they are," said Trevor.

As he played, someone behind the bandstand caught Fireman Sam's eye.

Norman had discovered his latest invention! Fireman Sam signalled for him not to give the game away.

Norman grinned. "I wish you could invent a machine to do my homework, Fireman Sam!" he whispered, and joined in the applause.

A Spot of Bother

It was the last day of term and Sarah and James were on their way to school.

"Hurry up, Norman," called James. "It's the best day of term, remember?"

"Not for me," mumbled Norman. "I've got to do the spelling test again."

"Hello you two, waiting for Norman as usual?" said Fireman Sam, who had come for his newspaper. "How

about a treat for break time?"

"Oo, yes please, Uncle Sam," the twins replied.

"Well, I never," said Dilys. "There's a chicken-pox epidemic in Pontypandy valley. Newspaper for you, Fireman Sam?" She folded up the paper she had been reading and handed it over.

"Oh er, thanks," said Fireman Sam.

"I'll have two of those chocolate bars for Sarah and James as well, please," he said.

"Where's Norman?" asked Sarah. "He was here a moment ago."

"Won't be long. Just learning my spelling," Norman shouted from upstairs.

"Mam, I've got spots!" cried Norman, racing downstairs.

"Ooo, my poor darlin'," cried Dilys. "It's that chicken-pox. I knew it, he's so sensitive. Look at all those spots!"

"Don't worry, Mam. I'll go to bed after school," Norman coughed feebly.

"You'll go upstairs right this minute!" ordered Dilys.

"We'd better go before we all catch chicken-pox too," shrugged James, looking at his watch.

"Hope you feel better soon, Norman!" called Fireman Sam as they all left the shop.

Up at the fire station, Elvis was giving Trevor his breakfast.

"Why don't you try some muesli, Trevor?" asked Penny. "It's much healthier."

"Thanks, Penny, but my appetite's healthy enough already!" said Trevor tucking into bacon and eggs.

"Right, here are the duties for today," said Station Officer Steele. "Fireman Sam, you're on call. Firefighter Morris, check food supplies. Cridlington and Evans . . . timed jogging. And no excuses!"

"But, Sir, lunch is just going into the oven – it'll burn," Elvis pleaded.

"Mmm, me too," Trevor agreed, scratching his head.

Norman giggled as Trevor and Elvis took the wrong turning.

"Let's stop here and wait for a bus," Elvis suggested when they came to a bus stop.

"It'll be a long wait, Elvis! I'm the bus driver, remember!" said Trevor. "But we may as well have a rest."

Meanwhile, as soon as Dilys was busy, Norman leaped out of bed and wiped his 'spots' off with a tissue. "I'm not wasting the day indoors!" he said.

He'd reached Pandy Lane when he saw two figures in the distance. They gave him an idea.

"That's odd," said Elvis, looking at the road sign and frowning. "I thought Pontypandy was that way."

They sat down and fell fast asleep.

"Now for some real fun," Norman whispered. Being careful not to wake them, he drew red spots on the sleeping firemen's faces.

"Glad I spotted you here! Hee hee!" he giggled to himself.

When Elvis and Trevor didn't come back, Fireman Sam and Station Officer Steele went to look for them.

"There they are, Sir," said Fireman Sam.

"Miles off course," muttered Station Officer Steele. "Whoever heard of a bus driver with no sense of direction!"

"Sir, they're covered in spots!" said Fireman Sam.

"In that case, they'll have to walk home. We can't risk infecting the whole force," Station Officer Steele said briskly.

Suddenly the alarm in Jupiter's cab sounded.

"Good heavens, there's a fire at the fire station," said Station Officer Steele, talking to Penny on the radio. "We need all hands to the pump for this one, spots or not. Into Jupiter everyone!"

With the siren blaring and the lights flashing, they raced through Pontypandy.

"Mamma mia! It's the fire station – it's burning down!" exclaimed Bella, pointing at the cloud of smoke.

"Oh help! It's the gas cooker," said Elvis, going pale as he saw smoke pouring from the kitchen window.

"I thought jogging was a bad idea – first chicken-pox and now this," said Trevor. "Never again!"

"Well, don't just stand there, get the hose," yelled Station Officer Steele.

"I'll switch off the gas at the mains first," said Firefighter Penny Morris.

Fireman Sam and Fireman Elvis Cridlington put on their air supply masks and picked up the hose. Kicking open the door, they charged into the smoke-filled kitchen.

"Stand by to help, this one looks serious," Fireman Sam reported back over the radio.

"How's it going, Fireman Sam?" asked Station Officer Steele a few minutes later.

"Send reinforcements," came the reply.

"In you go, Firefighter Morris," ordered Station Officer Steele. Penny grabbed a fire extinguisher and went inside.

Inside the kitchen, the three of them soaked the cooker in a flood of water.

"Coming under control at last, Sir," said Fireman Sam, as the flames died down, leaving the scorched cooker smouldering.

"Well, I won't be cooking on that for a bit, I suppose," said Elvis wiping his face. "Phew, it's hot in here."

"Some good news anyway," grinned Fireman Sam. "Elvis, wipe your face again."

"Aw," exclaimed Elvis, "chicken-pox all over my fingers!"

Later that day, Fireman Sam was in Dilys's shop when Norman came skipping in.

"I'm better now, Mam," he said cheerfully.

"Norman Price, you get back into bed at once with all those spots!" said Dilys.

"You won't wipe those off so easily, my boy," laughed Fireman Sam, as Norman scrubbed frantically at his face.

"And Mrs Williams says you can do the spelling test next term," said James.

"Mam," moaned Norman, "I feel ill!"

19

All in a Good Cause

Trevor Evans had been installing Bella's new shower and was just finishing reconcreting the pavement outside the café.

"There you are, Bella," he said, standing back to admire his work. "You're going to have the smartest shower in Pontypandy, even if I say so myself."

"Thanks to you, Trevor," Bella replied. "Come in for some dinner when you've finished, on the house."

"Ooo, yes please, Bella!" Trevor called.

"Look at this, Trev," said Fireman Sam. "£300 for the children's ward, all from the fire station raffle." He opened his briefcase.

"How about some raffle tickets?" called out Fireman Sam as he went into the café. He put his case down on an old box of rubbish.

"Thanks, Fireman Sam. I'll buy five," replied Bella, dumping some more rubbish on top of the pile. She'd been clearing out while Trevor installed her shower.

20

"Thanks, Bella," said Fireman Sam, giving Bella the tickets. "It's all in a good cause. We've raised £300 already." He picked up the case from the top of the boxes and left the café.

"Ciao, Fireman Sam," said Bella. She looked down, and frowned at the pile of rubbish. "But I thought . . ."

Up at the fire station, Elvis and Penny were admiring a large basket of fruit.

"That looks juicy," said Fireman Sam.

"Yes, Mrs Price has donated it as a raffle prize," Penny explained. "Isn't she kind?"

"Yuk! These are bad," said Elvis, spitting out a grape.

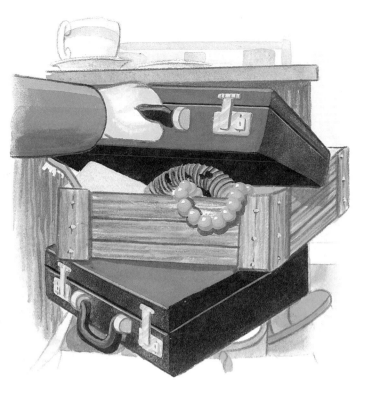

"Trust Dilys," sighed Fireman Sam.

"How's it going, Fireman Sam?" asked Station Officer Steele when he arrived.

"£300 so far, Sir, and we haven't finished yet. Could you look after the money while we do the charity bed push in Pontypandy this afternoon, please?"

"That's the spirit! Keep up the good work, Fireman Sam!" said Station Officer Steele.

21

"Oi, Mr Evans," said Norman cheekily, popping his head round the corner. "Can I write my name in the wet concrete?"

"Just you dare, Norman Price!" Trevor warned.

"How about a humbug then?" Norman offered Trevor the bag of sweets.

"Don't mind if I do," replied Trevor. Squelch! He stepped into the wet concrete!

Bella, meanwhile, was piling up her rubbish in the garden. "Time for a good bonfire. I don't need all this junk in my new bathroom - it's no good to anyone," she thought to herself.

"You can't trust public transport any more," Dilys grumbled as the charity bed push passed the bus stop. Penny rattled the bucket and Dilys dropped in a small coin.

"Seeing as you've paid your fare, Dilys, we'll give you a lift," Penny grinned.

Trevor was still concreting when they arrived outside the shop.

"That looks comfy, Dilys," he called.

"Yes, and it's more reliable than the bus service these days," retorted Dilys. "Thanks for the ride, Penny."

"That's interesting," Dilys thought, taking a good look at the rubbish Bella had heaped up for her bonfire. She poked around and pulled a couple of things out.

"It would be a shame to burn these - I'm sure I could use them."

Checking that no-one was looking, she scurried home.

When Fireman Sam got back to the fire station, Station Officer Steele looked worried. Fireman Sam's briefcase was open on his desk, empty!

"Now, Fireman Sam, where did you last see the money?" he asked.

"Um . . . oh yes, at Bella's this morning. She was clearing out rubbish. Quick!"

Bella carried the last load of rubbish outside and set fire to the pile.

"Mamma mia! I didn't know I had so much to throw away," she said as the fire blazed.

She heard the telephone ringing and hurried inside.

"Hello Fireman Sam. Don't worry about the smoke. It's only my bonfire."

"Bella, have you got a briefcase like mine? I think they've got mixed up."

"Zat old thing! I've just put him on the bonfire. Why?" The line went dead.

Elvis and Penny were sitting in the fire station mess when the alarm rang and Fireman Sam charged in.

"There's a fire at the café," he shouted. "Oh don't worry," said Penny, sitting down again. "Bella's having a bonfire, that's all."

"I know," said Fireman Sam, "and the briefcase, with the money for the children's ward inside, is on it!"

Grabbing their helmets, the crew jumped into Jupiter. With the siren blaring and the lights flashing, they roared off down the road towards the café.

Watched by Trevor, Jupiter screeched to a halt in the wet concrete outside the café. Dragging the hose, the firemen rushed round the back to the bonfire.

"What's going on at Bella's?" asked Norman, coming out of the shop to watch.

But it was too late. All that was left of Bella's pile of rubbish were a few smoking remains. And there was no sign of the briefcase!

"Well, that's it," said Fireman Sam. "£300 up in smoke. I'll never repay that."

"As it's for you, Bella, I'll have one last go at this job," Trevor agreed with a weary groan as he looked at the tyre marks in the wet concrete. "But, this is my last try - any more marks will have to stay."

He didn't see Norman grinning as he listened round the corner.

"What am I going to do?" groaned Fireman Sam. "How was I to know that Bella had a briefcase identical to mine? Now we'll have to start all over again."

Everyone was silent. Then, they heard hysterical screaming coming from across the street.

They raced outside to see Dilys waving her arms about.

"What's wrong Dilys?" Fireman Sam cried, forgetting all about the money as he rushed over to help.

"Nothing . . . but Fireman Sam! Look!"

Dilys was carrying a black briefcase and waving fistfuls of £5 notes!

"That's the raffle ticket money! Thank goodness for that," said Fireman Sam, heaving a sigh of relief. "Where did you find that briefcase?" he smiled.

"Ah, well, I er . . . noticed it on Bella's bonfire and I er . . ." Dilys mumbled, going pink. "Anyway, waste not, want not, I say."

"Too right, Dilys! You're a heroine!"

"That's it - until Bella gets her next new bathroom anyway," said Trevor, exhausted. "Now

for some Italian home cooking."

"Go and look at my masterpiece," he said to Fireman Sam and Bella when he'd finished eating.

They all trooped outside.

"Not bad," chuckled Fireman Sam, "but I'm not sure about the hair!"

"What the . . ." Trevor gasped, staring at the cartoon in the pavement. "That Norman gets everywhere!"

Lost in the Fog

"It's not fair, this isn't," moaned Norman, as he mopped the shop floor. "It was an accident . . . honest."

"Accident my foot!" Dilys scoffed. "I suppose those stink bombs just appeared out of thin air!"

"But Mam, I'm going to Penny Morris's for tea with Sarah and James . . ."

"No, Norman, you're not getting away with it this time."

Meanwhile, Fireman Sam and Elvis were driving back to Pontypandy after a call out.

"Cloud's coming down thick over the valley," said Fireman Sam, turning on Jupiter's headlights.

Later, Dilys was reading her horoscope at Bella's café.

"A load of rubbish zey are," said Bella.

"No they're not. I always read mine," said Dilys.

"I read the tea leaves too," she added peering into Bella's empty cup. "Mrs Lasagne," she said, "you will meet a dark handsome man who loves to travel."

Sarah, who had overheard Dilys, was impressed. "Tell my fortune, please, Mrs Price," she begged.

"I can't read tea leaves from milk shakes," said Dilys, "but . . . swill this cup out." She handed Sarah the cup she'd just finished with. "Ah . . . um, I see you going on a journey this afternoon," said Dilys.

"Wow! Go on, Mrs Price," urged James.

"To Newtown . . . oh dear, it's misting over now . . ."

"I think crystal balls do that, no, Mrs Price?"

asked Bella suspiciously, but as Trevor came into the café she joked, "Perhaps Mr Evans is my handsome travelling man!"

"What did I tell you?" said Dilys. "I've got the gift! And it looks as though you'll come to a sticky end, Sarah," Dilys continued, watching Sarah wipe the jam off her face with her hanky.

"Come on you two," said Trevor. "Time for us to go."

"Bye, Uncle Sam," called Sarah and James, waving as Jupiter passed Trevor's bus.

"Can we get out here, please?" asked Sarah, when they got up into the hills. "We want to pick some daisies for Penny."

Trevor looked at the cloud and frowned.

"Don't worry," said Sarah. "We can walk from here. It's not far to Newtown."

"All right then, but be careful," he called out. The twins had already climbed over the gate into the field.

"Hurry up Sarah, or we'll be late for tea," shouted James impatiently.

"Just a few more," called Sarah.

By now, the cloud had turned into fog. It was getting thicker and thicker.

Back at the shop, Norman was still cleaning. "I'm no good at this," he moaned as a sack of budgie seed toppled over.

"You need the practice then," said Dilys crossly. "If only I could have seen what the future held for me," she muttered.

"I bet Penny will take Sarah and James to the pictures after tea," said Norman with a sigh, as he picked up the mop again. "And here's me slavin' away at home!"

Dilys grinned to herself as she overheard what Norman was saying.

"There we are," said Sarah, holding up a big bunch of daisies. "Let's go."

"Yes, or we'll miss the film," James agreed. "Oh . . . I can't see the gate."

"Don't be such a baby, it's over there!"

"No, it's not," James replied nervously.

Sarah looked around. "Oh dear, you're right for once. Now what can we do?"

The twins wandered around, searching for the way back to the road.

"Aagh! What's that?" screamed Sarah.

"Only a tree, silly," whispered James. "Everything looks different in the fog – isn't it spooky?"

"Strange," said Penny, peering out of the window into the fog. "Sarah and James should be here by now. I'd better call Pontypandy and see what's happened."

"Well, I don't know, but I did see them in the bus with Trevor," said Fireman Sam when Penny rang.

"Newtown's hidden by fog," said Penny. "They must be lost."

"We'd better go and look for them," said Fireman Sam. "I'll meet you halfway along the Newtown road, Penny."

"Rightio, Sam. Drive carefully," said Penny and she set out in Venus.

"Fireman Sam to Firefighter
Penny Morris. Over," said Fireman
Sam as he drove slowly with Jupiter's
headlights on.

"I can't see much, Sam. Oh! Here
are some headlights."

"Hang on, Penny, here's a car!"
Fireman Sam slammed on the
brakes.

"Oh! It's Jupiter," exclaimed Penny.

The two vehicles stopped just in
time.

"Phew, that was lucky!" said Penny, jumping out of Venus.

"Very," agreed Fireman Sam. "Now,
where have Sarah and James got to?"

"Look," said Penny pointing to the
gate.

"Sarah's hanky," said Fireman Sam.
"They went through the gate. Right,
you stay with the vehicles while I go
and look." He picked up his torch and
set off.

"Sar-ah! Ja-ames! Where are you?"

Fireman Sam's voice echoed as he
made his way down the track in the fog.

"It's all your fault we're lost," James complained.

"No it's not!" Sarah argued as she stumbled forward. "Oh, help James!"

"You've fallen into the marsh! Quick, grab my hand," cried James.

"I'm going under!" cried Sarah.

"Don't panic Sarah. H-E-L-P!"

Fireman Sam stopped in his tracks.

"Sarah! James! I'm on my way," he called back. He started running in the direction of their cries.

"Great Fires of London! I can't go forward, or I'll sink too," said Fireman Sam.

"Any luck, Fireman Sam?" said Penny over the radio.

"We need your help. Drive down the track," Fireman Sam replied.

"Message received and understood. I'm on my way," said Penny calmly.

Penny drove Venus towards Sarah and fixed one end of a rope round the winch. She gave the other end to Fireman Sam.

"Right Sarah," said Fireman Sam, throwing the rope out to Sarah. "Catch the rope and put the loop under your arms."

They all waited nervously.

"Got it!" yelled Sarah, after a few tries.

"Well done," said Fireman Sam with relief. "Start winching, Penny."

Very slowly, the rope was pulled tight and eventually Sarah was pulled out of the boggy ground, into Fireman Sam's arms.

"Thanks, Penny," said James, and he handed Penny the bunch of daisies that Sarah had dropped.

Back at the café, Sarah and James were tucking into Bella's special pizza when Dilys walked in, followed by Norman.

"What are you two doing here? You're supposed to be at the pictures," exclaimed Dilys, surprised.

"How did you know that?" asked Sarah.

"Oh . . . I just know," Dilys sighed.

"I told you this morning, you mean," said Norman. "Remember, Mam?"

Dilys turned round and glared at Norman.

"Oh dear! Norman's future is looking dim!" giggled Sarah and they all laughed at the joke.

The Fairground Rescue

A fun fair had come to Pontypandy and everybody was enjoying themselves.
"I'll treat you ladies to a toffee apple," said Trevor to Dilys and Bella.
"Let's go on the helter skelter, Mam!" cried Norman.
"Not me!" replied Dilys. "Just the thought of it makes me go all dizzy."
"I'll take you, Norman," said Fireman Sam.
"Can we come too?" asked the twins.
"Of course," chuckled Fireman Sam. "Let's go."
On the way, Fireman Sam and the children stopped to buy ice-creams.
"Yummee! It's fantastic," drooled Norman, licking the drips round his cone.
"Last one to the top's a cissy!" cried Sarah, when they reached the helter skelter.

"Wheeee!" squealed the twins as they sped down the slide. Norman slid down so fast his ice-cream flew right out of the cone!

Meanwhile, Dilys and Bella were enjoying a ride on the ferris wheel.

"We're so high up people down below look like ants," said Dilys.

"Ah, bellissimo," sighed Bella. "I haven't done this since I was a little girl in Roma."

Down below, Fireman Sam suggested a ride on the roller coaster next.

"Brill!" replied Sarah.

"Why don't you come too, Trevor?"asked James.

"Not likely!" replied Trevor. "I can't stand heights. This is more my style!" he grinned, climbing onto a carousel horse.

As Trevor enjoyed his ride on the carousel, Fireman Sam and the children climbed aboard a roller coaster car.

"Hold on tight," said Sam as the car moved off slowly and began climbing a steep stretch of track.

"This is boring!" moaned Norman. "It's much too slow!"

Soon the car reached the crest of the track. Suddenly, it began speeding down the other side. Faster and faster it went!

"Whooa!" cried Norman.

"You don't seem so bored now, Norman!" laughed Fireman Sam.

"Wheeee!" squealed the twins. "This is brill Uncle Sam!"

Dilys and Trevor watched from below as Fireman Sam and the children raced up and down at high speed.

"What's happened?" asked Dilys.

"I'm not sure," said Trevor. "I'm going to check the control booth. You call the fire brigade!"

Trevor raced over to the control booth. It was just as he'd feared – the roller coaster had had a power failure and Sam and the children were stranded at the top!

The car reached the top of a hill, then suddenly stopped. Fireman Sam looked down at the cars at the bottom of the roller coaster. They weren't moving either.

On the ground below, Trevor and Dilys were puzzled.

From the top of the track, Fireman Sam could see Trevor beside the control booth.

"Great fires of London!" he cried. "I do believe there's been a power cut."

"But how will we get down?" asked James.

"Don't worry," said Sarah, "Uncle Sam's sure to think of something."

Sam frowned. All he could think of was to call the Pontypandy Fire Brigade. But how could he from the top of the roller coaster?

"Everybody stay very still until help arrives," said Fireman Sam.

"It's a l-long way down," gulped James.

"M- miles," stuttered Norman.

From down below, Trevor shouted, "Don't move, Sam. We've called the fire station!"

As Fireman Sam breathed a sigh of relief, Jupiter raced into the fun fair, followed closely by Venus, their lights flashing and sirens blaring.

"Jump to it!" commanded Station Officer Steele, as the engines screeched to a halt.

"Get the equipment from the lockers," ordered Station Officer Steele. "Firefighter Cridlington, we'll have to cordon off the area, and make sure the passengers in the cars at the bottom of the track get off safely!"

"Yes, sir!" replied Elvis.

Meanwhile, Firefighter Penny Morris began unloading ladders from Jupiter.

They leaned the ladders against the roller coaster. "It's no use," said Station Officer Steele. "Sam's car is too high for the ladders to reach."

"Why don't we lean them onto the lowest part of the roller-coaster and then use the catwalk?" suggested Penny.

"Good idea," replied Station Officer Steele.

The children watched nervously from the roller coaster car as Station Officer Steele and Firefighter Penny Morris began climbing the ladders.

"I wish they'd hurry. I don't like it up here," said Norman.

At last Station Officer Steele and Penny climbed onto the catwalk. A few minutes later they reached the car.

"Thank goodness," whispered James.

"Is everyone all right?" asked Penny.

The children nodded their heads.

Fireman Sam lifted the children out of the car one by one and the firefighters took them down the catwalk to safety.

"Is my brave little darling all right?" cooed Dilys anxiously as Norman reached the bottom of the ladder.

"Huh!" replied Norman. "I wasn't scared at all, Mam."

"Not much!" chuckled Sarah and James.

Sarah turned to Fireman Sam. "I knew you'd think of a plan, Uncle Sam."

"Me?" said Fireman Sam. "I didn't do anything. It was the quick thinking of Trevor and Dilys and the expert help of the Fire Brigade that rescued us."

"Thank you, everyone," said the children.

"I'll tell you one thing, I'll be keeping my feet on the ground from now on," added James.

"Excellent job," Station Officer Steele said proudly.

"Yes, I think everyone deserves a treat, Sir," said Sam. "And what better place to have one than a fun fair!"

"That's a grand idea," chuckled Station Officer Steele. "Let's have some fun!"

First, Station Officer Steele and Dilys had a ride on the log flume. Unfortunately, when their log landed in the pool it made a hugh splash and poor old Trevor got soaked!

"Let's go on the dodgems now!" cried Sarah and James.

"Not me!" chuckled Fireman Sam. "I've had quite enough excitement for one day!"

"And I'm too wet," moaned Trevor.

So Penny, Elvis and the children roared around in their dodgem cars, laughing as they bumped into each other.

Meanwhile, Fireman Sam wandered off to the snack kiosk and returned with a huge hot dog for Trevor. "Here you are, Trev. This may not dry you off, but it will certainly cheer you up," said Sam. "You deserve it."

"Thanks, Sam," said Trevor, licking his lips. "That's what I call the fun of the fair!"

Norman and the Runaway Cow

Fireman Sam was driving through the winding country lanes of Pontypandy. Elvis needed cabbage and potatoes to cook supper at the station.

"I'll ask Trevor for some fresh vegetables from his allotment," said Fireman Sam.

He drove along Pandy Lane until he arrived at Trevor's allotment.

As he climbed down from Jupiter, Fireman Sam saw Trevor racing around the allotment waving his hands above his head and shouting, "Shoo! Shoo!"

"Great fires of London!" cried Fireman Sam.

"What on earth are you doing, Trevor?"

"I'm trying to frighten the crows away!" moaned Trevor. "They're eating all my vegetables!"

"What you need is a scarecrow," said Fireman Sam.

"I've tried that," said Trevor. "The crows used it as a perch!"

Trevor took his spade and began digging up potatoes. "I can give you a nice sack of spuds," said Trevor, "but I'm afraid my cabbages are ruined!"

"Perhaps you could make me something to scare the birds away," said Trevor as Fireman Sam got ready to leave.

Fireman Sam went to Dilys Price's shop to buy a cabbage.

"What's the matter, Dilys?" he asked, pointing to the cotton wool in her ears.

"That's much better!" said Fireman Sam.

"Ah!" cooed Dilys. "He's a little genius!"

In the next room, however, Dilys's 'little genius' Norman, was sneaking out of the window.

"I'll leave that record of violin music playing," chuckled Norman. "Mam will never know I've gone!"

"Pardon?" said Dilys loudly.

Suddenly Sam heard an awful screeching noise. He clapped his hands over his ears.

Dilys smiled and removed the cotton wool. "My darling Norman is practising the violin. I tell him practice makes perfect, but I'm afraid he still has far to go."

"I'll say!" chuckled Fireman Sam as he picked a large cabbage.

Suddenly, beautiful violin music came wafting through the shop.

Back at the Fire Station, Elvis and Station Officer Steele were having a tea break.

Elvis was studying a recipe book. "Some great recipes here," he said to himself. "Hmm, perhaps I'll do a lemon meringue pie for pudding."

Fireman Sam walked in carrying the cabbage and potatoes.

"Great!" cried Elvis. "That's just what I need for my goulash with sour cabbage!"

"A simple roast dinner would do!" groaned Station Officer Steele.

By now, Norman was out at Pandy Farm carrying a lasso.

"Two-gun Norman Price is gonna rustle some steers," drawled Norman.

But when Norman saw Farmer Jones' cow, Daisy, he had second thoughts.

"Er, that's a big s-steer!" he said.

"Time to make tracks," gulped Norman as he scuttled away.

Unfortunately, when Norman ran out of the field, he forgot to close the gate behind him and Daisy wandered out.

At that moment, Firefighter Penny Morris was on her way to Pontypandy Fire Station in Venus.

As she came round a bend, she almost collided with Daisy who was crossing the road.

"Watch out!" cried Penny as she beeped the horn before swerving across the road.

Startled, Daisy gave a loud "Moo!" and ran off as fast as she could.

"I'd better get after her!" said Penny, climbing out of Venus.

Daisy lumbered across the wet fields until she lost her footing and slithered down the bank of a muddy stream. Daisy tried to climb out of the stream, but the more she struggled the more she became stuck.

"I'd better get help!" said Penny, when she saw what had happened. She hurried back to Venus to call the station. "Venus one to Pontypandy Fire Station, I need help to rescue a stranded cow, over," said Penny.

"Help on the way, over!" replied Station Officer Steele.

Fireman Sam and the crew sprang into action. Penny had just unloaded the winch and pulley from the rescue tender when they arrived.

"Let's get to work," said Station Officer Steele as Daisy mooed loudly.

"I'll use that tree as a hoist," said Penny.

As she attached the cable to the tree, Sam and Elvis waded into the stream to fasten the sling round Daisy. Frightened, Daisy mooed louder. Bit by bit, they winched her out of the mud.

"Easy, easy . . ." said Station Officer Steele. "That's it! Well done!"

"Good old Daisy!" said Penny. "Rescued, and without a scratch!"

"Plenty of mud, though," said Elvis.

"We'll soon get rid of that!" chuckled Fireman Sam, as he made for Jupiter. "All she needs is a little shower!"

As Fireman Sam gently hosed the mud from Daisy, she mooed with delight.

"I wonder how Daisy managed to get out of her field?" asked Penny.

Just then, Norman appeared from behind a bush.

"Stick 'em up, you critters!"

"Something tells me a certain little outlaw had something to do with it!" said Fireman Sam.

"If this was your fault Norman, the sheriff is going to take you back to town and toss you in the jailhouse!" drawled Fireman Sam.

"I didn't t-touch Daisy, honest!" replied Norman.

"You didn't close the gate behind you either," said Penny sternly.

Fireman Sam thought for a moment, then said, "I think it's time you had some more violin practice, Norman!"

Later, Fireman Sam and Trevor were sitting outside Trevor's allotment shed.

"I don't think you'll have a problem with the crows now," chuckled Fireman Sam as he handed a piece of cotton wool to Trevor. "Off you go, Norman!" he called.

A screeching, wailing noise split the air as Norman marched up and down playing his violin.

Trevor watched the crows scatter, then looked across at Fireman Sam. "I almost feel sorry for the birds," he chuckled.

Penny's First Aid Drill

Firefighter Penny Morris was at Pontypandy Fire Station to demonstrate first aid techniques. She watched with Station Officer Steele as Fireman Sam carried 'Henry', the dummy, down from the training tower.

"Easy does it, Fireman Sam," called Station Officer Steele.

"No problem, Sir," replied Fireman Sam.

Fireman Sam placed the dummy on the ground.

"Now I'll demonstrate how to apply artificial resuscitation," said Penny.

"It was called the 'kiss of life' in

my day," said Station Officer Steele.

"I'll volunteer!" Elvis piped up hopefully.

"Not you, Elvis," chuckled Penny, "I'll demonstrate on Henry!"

Meanwhile, Trevor Evans was preparing to paint Dilys Price's shop for her.

"It's overdue for a coat of paint, Dilys," said Trevor, studying the flaking paint on the stockroom window.

"I only had it painted ten years ago," sniffed Dilys.

"Well, nothing lasts nowadays, Dilys!" chuckled Trevor.

By midday, Trevor had begun removing the old paint from the window using a blowlamp and scraper.

Norman Price was in his bedroom up above when he spotted Trevor through his window.

"Now for some fun," he giggled as he grabbed his water pistol and aimed at Trevor.

Trevor had just lit his blowlamp and was softening the paint on the window frame. "This shouldn't take long," he said.

Just then, Norman squirted the top of Trevor's head with a jet of water.

"What on earth . . . ?" yelled Trevor, jumping back in surprise and dropping the blowlamp.

"Where did that water come from?" wondered Trevor as he peered up and down the street.

Inside the stockroom, the blowlamp had set alight a pile of empty cardboard boxes.

Trevor saw the smoke billowing through the window.

He ran inside the shop.

"Leave the shop and phone the fire brigade, Dilys," he shouted as he looked for the fire extinguisher. "Your stockroom's on fire!"

"Heavens!" cried Dilys. "I must get Norman!"

By the time Trevor returned to the stockroom it was really blazing.

"Come on Norman!" shouted Dilys. "We must get out at once. The shop's on fire!"

But Norman couldn't get

downstairs through the smoke.

"Oh no!" he cried. "What shall I do?"

Back at the fire station, the first aid demonstration was still going on.

"Elvis, you did want to volunteer, didn't you?" said Penny as she tied a sling around his neck. "Right, we'll bandage your head next."

"Ooh..ah..ooch!" wailed Elvis.

"You're a first-rate actor, Elvis!" laughed Penny. "Now, sit still."

Suddenly, Station Officer Steele burst in.

"Jump to it!" he ordered. "There's a fire at Dilys Price's shop!"

"What about my bandages?" asked Elvis.

"There's no time," replied Station Officer Steele. "Firefighter Morris will go instead."

Elvis watched forlornly as Penny climbed aboard Jupiter, followed quickly by Station Officer Steele and Fireman Sam.

"Right, Fireman Sam, let's go," said Station Officer Steele.

Jupiter sped towards Pontypandy, her siren blaring and lights flashing.

"Hurry Fireman Sam!" said Station Officer Steele. "If we're not quick, the whole of Pontypandy High Street will be on fire!"

"Hang on to your helmets!" replied Fireman Sam as Jupiter roared down the hill. Jupiter screeched to a halt outside the shop.

As the firefighters jumped down, they saw Trevor trying to fight the blaze with the fire extinguisher.

"Thank goodness you've arrived!" he exclaimed. "The fire's getting out of control!"

"And my Norman's trapped upstairs!" cried Dilys in a panic.

"Help, Mam!" wailed Norman from the bedroom window.

"Don't worry, Dilys," replied Fireman Sam, "we'll soon have Norman down safely."

While Penny set about rescuing Norman, Fireman Sam and Station Officer Steele uncoiled the hoses from Jupiter.

"We've arrived just in time, Sir," said Fireman Sam as he aimed a stream of water into the stockroom. "A moment later and the whole shop would have gone up in flames!"

Penny meanwhile had unloaded the ladder. She positioned it against the bedroom window sill.

"Help! Help!" cried Norman.

"My poor little darling!" wailed Dilys.

"Stay right there, Norman," called Penny, "I'm coming up to get you."

Quickly, Penny climbed up the ladder to reach Norman. With Penny's help he scrambled out of the window and onto her shoulder.

"Steady, Norman," she said as they inched down the ladder.

"Don't drop him!" cried Dilys anxiously.

Penny placed Norman gently down on the pavement.

"Are you all right, Norman?" she asked.

"All right?" clucked Dilys. "Poor thing's as white as a sheet. He'll have to go straight upstairs to bed."

"Not until the fire is out and the building is made safe again," said Penny.

Straight to bed? thought Norman. *That means no school this afternoon!* Norman moaned and closed his eyes.

"He's fainted, poor darling!" cried Dilys.

Just then Fireman Sam appeared. "Well, the fire's out," he said. "How's Norman?"

"He was fine, but then he suddenly fainted," said Penny.

"It's the shock, see," said Dilys.

"He may have inhaled some smoke," said Penny.

Not very likely, thought Sam. "Mm, I wonder..."

"In that case there's only one thing for it," he said. "You'll have to give him the kiss of life, Penny!"

Norman opened one eye.

"Kiss of life?" he echoed. He jumped to his feet, blushing at the thought.

"That was a quick recovery!" said Penny.

"Good thing, this first aid," chuckled Fireman Sam. "Cured in seconds!"

"There's a brave little darling!" said Dilys. "He takes after his mam."

"So all's well that ends well," said Fireman Sam. "How did the fire start in the first place?"

"I'm to blame," said Trevor. "I got squirted with water and dropped the blowlamp."

"Perhaps that had something to do with it," said Fireman Sam pointing to a water pistol sticking out of Norman's pocket.

"You little terror!" cried Dilys tweaking Norman's ear. "As you're fit and healthy, you can help me clear up the stockroom!"

"Aw, Mam!" wailed Norman.

As Norman was led off by Dilys, Fireman Sam and Firefighter Penny Morris packed up the hoses and made their way back to the station. They arrived to find Elvis sitting glumly in a mess of bandages.

"What's up, Elvis?" asked Fireman Sam.

"I haven't been able to cook the tea with my arm bandaged up!" moaned Elvis.

"Splendid!" said Station Officer Steele.

"In that case, it's supper at Bella's café," chuckled Fireman Sam. "Penny, I think this first aid training is a very good idea!"

James and the Well

Fireman Sam was on his way to work one morning when he saw Sarah and James.

"We're going to make a wish in the wishing well at Pandy Farm," said Sarah.

"Why don't you come with us, Uncle Sam?" asked James.

"Why not?" replied Fireman Sam. "I've got some time to spare today."

When they arrived at Pandy Farm, they each made a wish, then tossed their coins into the well.

The coins clinked against the rubble at the bottom of the dry well.

"Come on, you two," said Fireman Sam. "If you're quick, I'll treat you to an ice-cream at Bella's café."

"How did you know, Uncle Sam?" Sarah exclaimed. "That's just what I wished for!"

At Bella's, Fireman Sam ordered two large strawberry ice-creams for the

twins. "Thank you, Bella," they said. As Fireman Sam took the money from his pocket to pay, he realised that he hadn't just thrown some coins into the well.

"Daro!" he groaned. "I must have thrown my key into the wishing well!"

"I've got a spare key somewhere," muttered Fireman Sam as he left the café to go to work. "But where?"

"Poor Fireman Sam," said Bella. "It's usually me that loses my door key!"

"Hang on a minute!" said James suddenly. Something in Bella's kitchen had given him an idea. "I know a way we can get Uncle Sam's key back."

James darted out of the door tugging Sarah along behind him.

Firefighter Penny Morris had gone to Pontypandy early that morning. She was showing Station Officer Steele the equipment she carried on Venus, the rescue tender.

"I've got all the latest rescue gear," said Penny. "There are winches, cutters and even an inflatable air bag."

When Fireman Sam arrived, Penny was demonstrating the air bag to Station Officer Steele. Penny pressed a switch on Venus. The bag began to fill with air.

"It's used for rescuing people trapped under a vehicle," said Penny. "As the bag inflates, it lifts the vehicle so we can reach the people underneath."

"Very impressive," said Fireman Sam.

"Humph!" snorted Station Officer Steele. "What's wrong with a bit of old-fashioned elbow grease?"

Back at the wishing well, James was tying a magnet to his fishing rod. "I got the idea in Bella's café," he said. "She has magnets on her fridge to hold important notes."

Sarah could see the key at the bottom of the well.

"There it is!" she cried.

James played out the fishing line, slowly lowering the magnet into the well.

"Almost there," he said, stretching over the well. The line didn't quite reach, so James leaned over even further. "I've got —" he started to say, but then lost his balance and toppled into the well!

"James!" Sarah called. "James, are you all right?"

"I th-think so," called back James, his voice echoing around the well.

"I can't reach you," said Sarah. "I'll phone Uncle Sam. He'll know what to do."

"Action stations!" shouted Station Officer Steele when the message came through at the Fire Station. "James is trapped in the well at Pandy Farm! Firefighter Cridlington, you stay here to mind the phone!"

"I'll follow you!" called Penny Morris as Fireman Sam and Station Officer Steele drove off in Jupiter.

Fireman Sam drove Jupiter along the winding country lanes. It was raining now, and the roads were wet and slippery. As they came round a bend, Jupiter swerved across the road, skidding on the wet surface, and slid into a ditch.

Penny pulled up alongside as Fireman Sam and Station Officer Steele climbed out of the cab.

"Are you all right, Sam?" asked Penny.

"Er, nothing broken," said Fireman Sam.

"You'll have to give us a lift, Firefighter Morris," said Station Officer Steele as he adjusted his helmet. "We'll sort out Jupiter once we've rescued James."

A few minutes later they arrived at the wishing well in Venus, the rescue tender.

"Don't worry, James," Sam called into the well. "We'll have you out in no time."

"Fireman Sam and I will lower you into the well with a rope," Station Officer Steele told Penny. "Then we'll pull you and James to safety."

"There's no need, Sir," explained Penny. "We can use the electric winch on Venus."

Penny uncoiled a cable and harness from the back of the tender and fed it over the wooden beam of the well.

Then she climbed into the cab and started the engine. She pressed a button and the cable slowly lowered the harness into the well.

Penny switched off the power and Fireman Sam called to James, "Put on the harness and buckle it tight."

When Sam gave her the signal, Penny switched the generator back on and James was hoisted up the well.

"This is brill!" chuckled James as he slowly rose to the surface.

"Can I have a go, too?" asked Sarah.

"Not likely!" said Fireman Sam as he helped James out of the well. "We'll make sure this well has a grid fitted in future!"

"How did you manage to fall down the well, James?" asked Fireman Sam.

"I was trying to get this back for you, Uncle Sam," replied James, pulling a small metal object from his pocket.

"My door key!" chuckled Sam. "Thank you, James."

"That's a very useful piece of equipment, Firefighter Morris," said Station Officer Steele as Penny reloaded the cable and harness onto Venus.

"Thank you, Sir," beamed Penny. "Climb aboard and I'll give you and Fireman Sam a lift back to Jupiter."

As they stopped alongside Jupiter, Station Officer Steele said, "Come on, Fireman Sam, let's get stuck in. We've got to get Jupiter upright somehow. We'll have to go round the other side and push."

"Why don't you try the air bag, Sir?" suggested Penny.

"Nonsense!" scoffed Station Officer Steele. "I'm sure we can manage without such contraptions."

Fireman Sam and Station Officer Steele pushed and pulled for all they were worth, but they couldn't budge Jupiter.

"Perhaps we should give the air bag a try," panted Station Officer Steele.

Penny placed the air bag underneath Jupiter and switched on the air hose. Slowly the bag inflated, pushing Jupiter upright again.

"Bravo!" cried Fireman Sam.

"Hardly a scratch," said Fireman Sam as he examined Jupiter.

Station Officer Steele congratulated Penny as she loaded the air bag onto Venus.

"You're quite right, Firefighter Morris," he said. "There's a lot to be said for modern equipment after all."

"Yes, Sir," said Fireman Sam as he reached into the cab of Jupiter. "But there's one piece of old-fashioned equipment every firefighter should have."

"What's that?" asked Penny.

Sam chuckled as he filled their cups. "A nice, hot flask of tea!"

Stories first published in Great Britain 1991, 1992
by Buzz Books, an imprint of Reed Children's Books
Michelin House, 81 Fulham Road, London SW3 6RB
and Auckland, Melbourne, Singapore and Toronto

This edition published 1993 by Dean,
in association with Heinemann Young Books
Reprinted 1994, 1996

Fireman Sam © copyright 1985 Prism Art & Design Limited
Text © copyright 1991, 1992 Reed International Books Limited
Illustrations © copyright 1991, 1992 Reed International Books Limited
Stories by Caroline Hill-Trevor and Rob Lee
Illustrations by The County Studio
Based on the animation series produced by Bumper Films for
S4C/Channel 4 Wales and Prism Art & Design Limited
Original idea by Dave Gingell and Dave Jones, assisted by Mike Young.
Characters created by Rob Lee.

Produced by Mandarin Offset
Printed and bound in China

ISBN 0 603 55103 3

A CIP catalogue record for this book is available in the British Library.